THE
VEGETARIAN TROLL

Also by Ralph Wright

The Shrivelling Secret
The Witch's Big Toe
The Witch's Funny Bone
The Witch Goes for Gold

THE VEGETARIAN TROLL

RALPH WRIGHT

Illustrated by Cathy Simpson

MAMMOTH

First published in Great Britain 1990
by Methuen Children's Books Ltd
Published 1992 by Mammoth
an imprint of Mandarin Paperbacks
Michelin House, 81 Fulham Road, London SW3 6RB

Mandarin is an imprint of the Octopus Publishing Group,
a division of Reed International Books Ltd

Text copyright © 1990 Ralph Wright
Illustrations copyright © 1990 Cathy Simpson

ISBN 0 7497 0629 5

A CIP catalogue record for this title
is available from the British Library

Printed in Great Britain
by Cox & Wyman Ltd, Reading, Berkshire

Contents

1 A Riddle for the O'Briens 7

2 A Shock for Jago 14

3 The Vegetarian Troll 23

4 The Clean and Tidy Troll 33

5 The Well-dressed Troll 42

6 The Very Polite Troll 54

7 A Proper Troll 66

8 Good News and Bad 75

9 A New Lair 84

A Riddle for the O'Briens
1

'What's green and furry?' said Daniel.

Dawn looked at her twin brother. He was kneeling by the window with his nose squashed up against the pane. Not another of Daniel's riddles! Dawn was sick of hearing them! She decided to ignore him.

'Who's listening to this story, then?' asked Mrs O'Brien, tucking her legs up on the settee. Dawn snuggled close to her mother, but Daniel wanted to stay by the window.

'I've heard it before,' he said.

'I know!' his mother laughed. 'I wish I'd a pound for every time I've read it to you! But it's Dawn's favourite.' She flicked through the story book to find the page. 'Are you sure you won't sit with us, Daniel?'

'I can listen from here,' he answered, cross-legged on the floor.

So the twins' mother began the story.

'. . . when the three Billy-goats Gruff looked across to the other side of the river, the daisies looked bigger and juicier, and the grass looked greener. But the only way across the river was by the bridge, and under the bridge lived a great big ugly old troll . . .'

'What's green and furry,' said Daniel from the window, 'with eyes as big as saucers?'

'Oh, no, not again,' groaned Dawn.

'Why don't you pull the curtains, dear?' said Mrs O'Brien. 'It's getting dark.'

Daniel drew the curtains together, but he left a gap for himself and kept on looking out.

Mrs O'Brien read on till she came to the bit where the first billy-goat trots down to the river. '. . . and Little Billy-goat Gruff skipped on to the bridge, trip-trap, trip-trap, and when he was half way across, there came a voice: "Who's that trip-trapping across MY bridge?"'

'It's the troll!' said Dawn. 'He doesn't eat

the billy-goat, though, does he?'

'No,' smiled her mother. 'Don't worry.'

'I feel sorry for that troll,' said Daniel. 'He only wants his lunch.'

The story went on, and sure enough the little billy-goat got away. Then the second goat came down to the bridge.

'"... I'm coming up to eat you," said the troll. "Oh, don't eat me," said Middle Billy-goat Gruff. "My brother's coming along soon, and he's twice the size of me. His tail alone could feed you for a week!" "Ho! Really?" growled the troll. "Then I'll wait ..."'

'What's green and furry with eyes as big as saucers,' Daniel interrupted again, 'and a long pointy nose?'

'Oh, shush, Daniel,' said his sister. 'We don't want to hear your joke.'

'Can we please get on with the story?' begged Mrs O'Brien. 'It's nearly bedtime, you know. And don't think I've finished my work when I've got you two off to bed! I've still got to go and check next door.'

Mrs O'Brien had been asked to keep an eye on the next-door house while their neighbour, Mr Wise, was away in Australia.

'Go on, Mum – we're listening.' So the children settled down again and, as it got darker outside, it seemed cosier inside by the fire and now and again a breeze blew in the little top window that was open and made the curtain belly out. Soon Mrs O'Brien reached the end of the story.

'. . . and Great Big Billy-goat Gruff lowered his curly horns and charged at the ugly old troll, and tossed him right off the bridge, and he came down splash into the water, and he was never seen again. And now it *is* bedtime,' said Mrs O'Brien.

'Poor old troll!' said Daniel indignantly. 'He didn't get any food at all.'

'He shouldn't have tried to eat the billy-goats,' said Dawn.

'That's just what trolls *do*,' argued Daniel. 'He can't help being a troll, can he?'

Dawn was looking at the picture in the story book. 'The troll doesn't look fierce. He looks quite friendly. I wouldn't mind meeting a troll.'

'He might eat *you*,' grinned her brother. 'He'd crunch you up in no time!'

Dawn thought about it. 'No, he wouldn't,' she said at last. 'Not if he was a vegetarian.'

The others laughed. 'A vegetarian troll!' said their mother. 'What a funny idea!'

'Well, there might be some! Some people are vegetarians and eat no meat. Mr Wise next door, for instance! So why not trolls?'

'I don't know if there are any trolls nowadays, let alone vegetarian ones,' smiled her mum. 'Mind you, Mr Jenkins the farmer has lost some billy-goats lately, and he's looking for the culprit! Now, what was I saying about bedtime?'

Daniel had turned back to the window. 'What's green and furry, with eyes as big as saucers, a long pointy nose,' he said, 'and far too many teeth?'

Mrs O'Brien said to Dawn, 'I suppose

11

we'd better ask him. Or we'll never get any peace!'

'All right,' sighed Dawn. 'What *is* green and furry, with whatever kind of eyes and nose you said and far too many teeth?'

And they waited for the funny answer and then for Daniel to curl up in delighted laughter as he usually did.

But to their surprise he turned to them with a perfectly serious face.

'*I* don't know,' he said. 'I thought you might know. Because whatever it is . . . there's one at the bottom of the garden!'

They stared at him. Then they rushed to the window and pulled back the curtains in time to glimpse a strange, greenish shape disappearing through the hedge.

A Shock for Jago
2

Jago slipped out through the rose-hedge at the bottom of the O'Briens' garden. He never noticed the thorn catching in his green fur as he wriggled through, so he didn't miss the little tuft of it that got left behind.

Moving at a steady lope he soon crossed the sports field, pushed between the bushes that grew at the far side and set off uphill towards Windy Moor.

Hearing that billy-goat story through the open window had given Jago quite a shock.

It isn't nice to find you are the villain in a story!

An hour ago he had been quite happy to be the kind of creature he was. Proud of it!

Now he wasn't so sure.

If you could choose what kind of creature you wanted to be, thought Jago, maybe he'd have been something different. Perhaps a lion, or an eagle. Or a child like Daniel or Dawn.

But you can't choose. You're stuck with being what you are.

And he wasn't an eagle or a lion. Or a child.

He was a troll.

His mother Frith was a troll, his father Obrak was a troll, and *he* was a troll. And that was that.

In fact, he was a perfectly cheerful and happy troll, a normal, muddy, untidy young troll, an ordinary, lively noisy young troll.

Well, there was *one* thing different about Jago.

Most trolls kept away from people. The old trolls said: 'People and trolls do not mix,' and shook their shaggy heads wisely. But Jago, playing up on the moor, would look down on the town and wonder about the people he could see scuttling busily in and out of their lairs. Why couldn't people

15

and trolls mix? Why shouldn't they be friends? What would it be like to visit one of their lairs?

Jago started exploring near the town, to see what kind of creatures people were. Today he'd spotted two children playing in one of the gardens. Jago kept out of sight but he peered through the hedge. He smiled to see the children rush in and out of a summer-house, swing on a swing, climb on a climbing-frame and on the apple trees.

He soon found out their names, when they called to each other.

'Daniel!'

'Dawn!'

'I want to play, too,' said Jago to himself. What fun they were having! On the moor he had nobody to play with. Not a single troll his own age lived there. In a minute he would call out to the children: 'Hello! I'm Jago! Can I play with you?'

But he didn't, because he didn't feel quite brave enough yet.

And while he was trying to get brave, the children's mother came out of the house and called them in.

Disappointed, Jago watched them go, and then he pushed through the hedge and crept up the garden. Perhaps he would

16

knock on the window?

A good thing he hadn't!

Because that was when he heard that bedtime story of theirs, and found out just in time that the O'Briens didn't like trolls at all.

They thought trolls were horrible, ugly creatures! They had eyes as big as saucers and far too many teeth. They lived under hump-backed bridges, getting ravenously hungry and leaping out on unwary billy-goats, eager to eat them up.

Jago shuddered to think of the ending of the story, when the troll was tossed in the river, never to be seen again. When he heard *that* Jago set off down the garden to go home, feeling quite upset. For although it may be a happy ending for a billy-goat, it's a very sad ending if you happen to be a troll.

Now Jago was out on the open moor. With his big eyes, he could see quite well in the dark. He lollopped along in that shambling, shuffling walk that trolls have. After a while he felt tired, so he stopped for a rest in a gorse bush.

Jago began to get over the shock. Now he knew the children didn't like trolls he was glad he hadn't spoken to them today. But

maybe he could change their minds . . .

The troll scratched behind his ears with rather dirty claws, got up on his hind legs, began loping across the moor again, and started to think.

Soon, a plan came into his head. The plan was: to invite the O'Briens to tea to meet his family!

Ah! There ahead was the family hump-backed bridge. Home at last!

'Ho-ho, Jago,' said a quavery voice from the stream.

'Ho-ho, Grandma,' said Jago. 'Where is everybody?'

'Not back yet,' said Grandma, and carried on wallowing in the mud.

Good! thought Jago. He went to his secret hidey-hole, pulled out the loose brick, and thrust a paw inside. He drew out a stub of a pencil and a scrap of paper. He sat on the bank and began to write by the light of the moon.

Deer Missers Obryen,
Plees cum to tee with us
at the bridj. Meat my Grandmar, she is
a nice oald lady trole.

Jago frowned. What would the O'Briens think of his Grandma spending all day in her mud-hole? He had an idea it wasn't what humans were used to. Better not mention Grandma, he decided. He crossed that bit out.

Granfather is a kynd and ermewsing oald chap. He is a bit dotty coz of being so oald, but he's still the ekspert at leeping out from under bridjis and skaring peeple off.

Jago sighed. It was very useful, Grandfather keeping strangers away from the lair, but that was just the kind of thing to put the O'Briens right off coming! He crossed that out, too.

My mum and dad will giv yoo a grate
welcum. Dad is big and strong with
hansum fangs and a fyne fierce fase –

Oh, no! Jago suddenly saw what Daniel and Dawn would make of *that*. They'd think his dad was a great big ugly troll like the one in the story, fit to frighten them to death!

For tee mum will make yoo the taystiest
billy-gote pye yoo ever hadd.

He groaned. He had remembered that eating billy-goats was the very thing that upset people the most! He crossed *that* out, too! Now there was nobody else to write about but baby Korta, and nothing to say about *her* except that she could cry, and that even she could eat her share of billy-goat as long as it was well mashed up.

It was hopeless!

Jago screwed up the whole letter and threw it away. He put his head between his paws in dismay. He had found out

something terrible.

Everything the people said about trolls was perfectly TRUE!

They *were* frightening creatures with unpleasant habits like goat-stealing and jumping out at travellers and wallowing in mud under bridges! And there was nothing he could do to change it.

That was the end of his dream of making friends with the children.

Or was it?

He sat on the bank for a long time in deep thought.

Only after a lot of water had gurgled its

way under the bridge, only then a glimmer of hope shone in the young troll's saucer-sized eyes. He had thought of another plan.

He couldn't change all the trolls – but he could change himself.

He could become a troll fit to have human friends!

And he'd make a start right now.

What was the troll's worst habit as far as the O'Brien family were concerned? No doubt about it! Catching billy-goats to eat!

All right; he'd stop eating billy-goat.

He had heard of some folks who didn't eat meat. What did they call them?

Vegetarians.

Right. He would become one of those.

Jago smiled happily as he heard the sounds of his mum and dad and grandfather returning home, splashing their way downstream to the lair.

The Vegetarian Troll
3

Frith gazed fondly at her son. How handsome Jago was, with his rich green fur, his eyes as big as saucers, his fine sharp nose, and his dear little fangs curling over his bottom lip in that cute way! She was so proud of him.

But Jago really was being most awkward about his food this morning! 'Do eat it up, Jago, I'm ready to clear away.'

'I told you, Mum, I can't eat this any more.'

'Can't eat it? That's best billy-goat pie, that is! Is it too hot? Too cold? Too tough and chewy for you?'

Jago shook his head. He'd tried to explain

about giving up billy-goat, but his mother didn't seem to get the point of it at all! He smiled at her, for he loved her very much. But he didn't eat his billy-goat pie.

The morning sun angled into the trolls' lair, brightening everything up, but it cast no light on the puzzle for Frith. She was baffled. She called for Grandma Troll. Perhaps *she* would know what to do.

There was a mighty sucking noise as Grandma heaved herself out of the mud-hole. This was a place at the bend of the stream, where the water ran slow and the mud was nice and thick. Grandma struggled every day to keep it clear of sharp, painful pebbles. Now she waded over towards the cave. Mud slithered off her fur and landed in wet slaps on the river bank.

'What's so important?' asked Grandma. 'I was just getting comfortable!'

'It's Jago – he won't eat his billy-goat pie!'

Grandma shuffled over to give Jago a muddy hug. 'What's up, Jago? You can tell your old Grandma.'

'It's all right, Grandma. I'm giving up billy-goat, that's all.'

'Giving up – ?' Grandma blinked. 'That doesn't make sense! It's as if I said, I'm

giving up mud-baths! Unthinkable. Impossible!'

Jago was puzzled. 'What have mud-baths got to do with it, Grandma?'

'It all comes down to mud in the end,' said Grandma wisely. 'Everything *does*.

And speaking of mud-baths, I was in the middle of the most delicious one just now. Excuse me!'

'Just a minute!' said Frith. 'What about Jago's food?'

Grandma paused on her way back into the stream. 'I expect it's just a phase he's going through,' she said.

'Oh! What's a phase? Is it catching?' asked Frith, bewildered. But Grandma was already sinking into the cool, slithery mud, sighing with pleasure at the feel of it, all over her leathery old skin. Jago watched until only her pointy nose and a few blue-green tufts of fur showed above the ripples at the water's edge.

'Oh, Jago, what a worry you are to your poor mother,' said Frith. 'Fancy catching a nasty phase!' Jago smiled at her again, but he still didn't eat his billy-goat pie.

Grandfather Troll came shambling along the river bank. He'd been hard at work leaping out at anyone who came too near the lair and scaring them away. He was very good at it because of his fierce, grizzled old face. He ducked under the arch of the hump-backed bridge. There, where the brickwork was crumbly, the troll family had dug out the cave to make their cosy lair.

Grandfather, his blue-grey fur dappled with worn patches, grinned cheerily at Frith as she sat in the lair, worrying.

'Oh, Grandfather,' she said. 'Jago won't eat his billy-goat pie. Grandma says he's got a phase.'

'Nonsense,' said Grandfather, after a quick look to make sure Grandma wasn't listening. 'A fellow can get fed up with billy-goat pie, that's all. It's perfectly natural. Phases don't come into it.' He winked at Jago.

'So what's the right thing to do, then?' said Frith, glad there was someone as wise as Grandfather around.

'Easy!' said Grandfather. 'Give him billy-goat stew instead!'

Jago stared at his grandfather, and shook his head.

'No?' The old troll tried again. 'Billy-goat chops, then?'

Again Jago shook his head.

Grandfather Troll went through a list of all the tasty dishes he could think of. Barbecued billy-goat, goatburgers, goat and fried bulrushes, goat nuggets in breadcrumbs, but each time, Jago shook his head.

Grandfather raised his shaggy eyebrows.

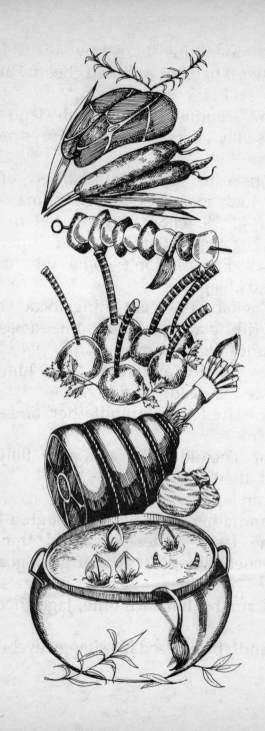

'Dear me,' he said. 'You're hard to please, young Jago. That's all the food I can think of. What *else* is there?'

Jago explained about the good things to eat you could find in the woods – Grandfather just looked blank and scratched the worn patches in his blue-grey fur.

'Whatever will your father say?' fretted Jago's mother.

There came a heavy step at the mouth of the cave. Jago's father Obrak had returned. His great bulk filled the little cave. His huge fangs gleamed. His magnificent tail lashed from side to side.

He kissed his wife, ruffled Jago's fur and took a peep at baby Korta asleep in the back of the lair. Then he noticed the glum faces of his family. 'Cheer up! The bridge hasn't fallen down yet, has it?' he joked.

'It's Jago!' wailed Frith. 'He won't eat his billy-goat pie!'

'Come now, Jago,' said her husband sternly. 'Eat it up at once.'

'But, Dad – I'm giving it up!'

'Giving *what* up?'

'Billy-goat. I'm going to be – a vegetarian!'

'A *what?*' bellowed Obrak, so loudly that

little Korta woke, and even Grandma climbed squelchily out of her mud-hole and came to see what was up.

'A vegetarian?' roared Obrak. Then he turned to his wife and muttered, 'What exactly *is* a vegetarian?'

Frith explained that it was something to do with not eating meat. Obrak looked baffled. He took some deep, shuddering breaths, to try to get a hold on himself. Then he went and squatted by Jago. He put a big, shaggy arm round his son's shoulders.

'Listen, son,' he said gently. 'It's time I explained some things to you.' He cleared his throat, not used to making speeches. 'Look around you. What do you see? Trolls! We are all trolls here. You are a troll. Trolls eat billy-goat. *All* trolls eat billy-goat. Always have and always will. So forget this nonsense and eat up your pie, eh? After all – what else *is* there to eat?'

'Well – nuts, and berries, and leaves!' said Jago.

'Leaves?' Jago's father looked helplessly round at the others for support. 'Is that food? Can you actually eat that stuff?'

'Not likely,' shuddered Grandfather Troll. 'Weird idea.'

'You would turn into a squirrel,' said Grandma. 'Or a rabbit.'

'See, Jago,' said his dad. 'There's no future in it. Eat your pie and be done with it!'

'But I don't *like* billy-goat!' cried Jago.

Obrak groaned. 'Oh, the shame of it! To think that a son of mine should turn into a vegetable – '

'Vegetarian, dear,' Frith put him right.

'Billy-goat was good enough for my father, and his father before him. It doesn't bear thinking about!' Obrak raged.

Jago felt miserable. He didn't want to go against his dad. Or turn into a squirrel. But it was time he stuck up for himself. He was old enough to choose his own food! Besides, it was all part of his plan to make friends with the children. He couldn't give in at the very first difficulty.

'All right,' he said in a small voice. 'I can see there's no room for a vegetarian troll in this family.' They all nodded at him. 'So . . . there's only one thing to do.'

He looked round at their faces as they waited for him to finish.

Jago swallowed. 'I shall have to leave home!' he said.

The Clean and Tidy Troll
4

'But where will you go?' said Frith.

She was helping Jago gather food – *his* kind of food – in the woods. Jago hadn't changed his mind about leaving home. He was determined to go that very day.

The young troll reached for a juicy bunch of leaves and thought about her question.

'I shall go to town, Mother!'

Frith looked startled. 'To town? But the people live there!'

'I'll make friends with them,' said Jago.

'You know what the old ones always say – people and trolls don't mix!'

'Perhaps it's time they did,' said Jago. 'Only yesterday I saw some children with their mother, who looked very friendly. I wanted to play with them. I found out that they don't like trolls, but I plan to change their minds!'

'How will you do that?' asked his mother, breaking off a sprig full of berries.

'I don't know,' admitted Jago. 'But the people in town will know! They are bound to know how to make friends with children. They are the ones to ask.'

'Well, be careful,' sighed Frith. Then she thought of another problem. 'Where will you *live?*'

'Don't worry,' said Jago. 'There will be lots of bridges in town.'

'I suppose so. All these new things! Being a vegetarian! Going to town! Talking to people!' She shook her head. 'Be sure not to forget you're a troll!'

Jago laughed. 'How could I ever forget that?'

He wrapped all the food they had collected into a cloth and tied up the corners around a stick, so that he could carry it. He was ready to go.

'I must get back to Korta,' said Frith.

Jago gave her a hug. 'I'll be all right, Mother, you'll see!'

'When you've found some friends and a

comfy bridge, come back and tell me all about it!'

'I will,' promised Jago. He turned and started along the path to town, lollopping the way trolls do. Every little while he turned and waved until Frith was out of sight.

What a great adventure! thought Jago. How would he get on in the world of people? He could hardly wait to find out!

When Daniel O'Brien found the piece of green fur in the hedge he ran inside and showed it to Dawn and his mother. 'This proves it!' he said in excitement. 'It really *was* a troll we saw last night!'

Mrs O'Brien was doubtful. 'We might have imagined it.' She frowned. 'We were reading a troll story – perhaps that made us *think* we saw a troll.'

'You both saw him, too!' Daniel protested.

'Only a *glimpse* of something,' said Dawn. 'Could have been anything!'

'Such as?' said Daniel scornfully.

'A fox, maybe?'

'A *fox*? A *green* fox? On its hind *legs*?'

Dawn took the tuft of green fur from her brother and stroked it. A picture crept into her mind of the creature who had left it behind . . . it *must* have been a troll! What else could it be?

'Just think!' she breathed. 'If we were the first to discover a troll for hundreds of years!'

'It *would* be exciting,' Mrs O'Brien agreed, 'but I'm very much afraid that, even if there used to be trolls, there's no such thing now!'

But Daniel had watched it in the garden; and Dawn had the bit of green fur; and the children just *knew* it had been a troll. From now on, they would keep their eyes open, hoping for another sighting of the creature.

The first bridge Jago found was a little footbridge at the edge of town. It crossed a stream that ran right through the middle of a supermarket car-park.

The troll looked doubtfully at the bridge. How could you dig a lair under it? The banks of the stream were concrete! It wasn't even hump-backed, it was flat. Not much of a bridge, thought Jago! But it would have to do for a start.

He jumped down into the pebbly stream and went and sat under the bridge. He munched a few leaves and felt better. After all, it was his very first bridge since leaving home. He felt quite proud of himself.

A little girl came along through the car-park, making her way to the bridge. She had her hair in a pony-tail and carried a bright red bag over her shoulder.

Oho! thought Jago. Here comes someone to ask about making friends. I will introduce myself in the usual troll way.

So, as soon as the little girl set foot on the bridge, Jago leaped up with a roar of, 'Who's that trip-trapping across MY bridge?'

'Ooh!' cried the girl in surprise. 'It's only me – Gaye!' And she added, when she saw Jago's sharp teeth, 'Please don't eat me!'

'Don't be silly,' laughed Jago. 'I don't eat children. In fact I don't eat meat at all – I'm a vegetarian. I only wanted to ask you a question.'

'All right,' said Gaye, feeling much better now she knew the creature wasn't going to eat her.

'I'm a troll who wants to make friends with two children,' said Jago. 'But they don't seem to like trolls. What should I do?'

Gaye swapped the bag over to her other shoulder and thought about it. 'Well, for a start,' she said, eyeing Jago's fur, 'I'd clean myself up, if I were you.'

Jago looked down at himself in dismay. He *was* muddy. Extremely muddy. In fact, he was covered with mud from head to toe.

'Don't you ever have a bath?' asked Gaye.

'Oh, yes – I often have a mud-bath,' said Jago.

Gaye laughed. 'That won't do! You must have a proper wash with clean water and soap.'

'Soap? What's that?'

Now Gaye was on her way to stay with her Aunty Bettina and she'd brought all her things. She took a bar of soap out of her shoulder bag. 'Here – try it!' she said.

So Jago jumped into the stream and began to wash with the soap. At first he

thought you were supposed to eat it, but Gaye explained that you should rub it all over yourself.

The troll was amazed to see so much mud come out of his fur, leaving it a bright, emerald green. He couldn't remember ever being quite so green before!

'*Much* better,' said Gaye, leaning over the rail of the little bridge. 'I have to go now, but here's a brush for you to brush your fur, and here's something to make you smell nice.'

Jago reached up to take them. 'You're very kind,' he said.

'It's all right,' said Gaye. 'I've got loads more. Goodbye, and good luck!'

What a friendly, helpful person! thought Jago, when the little girl had gone. I'm glad I met her. Now I know that if I'm to make friends with Daniel and Dawn, I must be clean and tidy.

Jago went for a walk to dry off. Away from town he found a quiet place and started to brush his fur. Soon he got the hang of it and, once he knew which end of the brush to hold, it wasn't long before his fur was tidy and smooth all over.

He opened the little bottle Gaye had given him. A *very* strong smell came out, a smell like flowers. 'Now what am I supposed to do with this?' he wondered. In the end he shrugged, tipped the bottle upside-down over his head and waited till the stuff had all gurgled out, trickling down his front and back. He could hardly breathe for the fumes. He hoped he had done the right thing. Anyway, after half an hour or so he got so used to the smell he didn't notice it any more.

'Time to get back to my bridge!' said Jago. On the way he found that it was one thing to *get* clean and tidy, another thing to *keep* that way! Bramble bushes kept wanting to catch on his beautiful fur and muddy puddles seemed to get under his feet on purpose, eager for Jago to splash or slip in them. He never *used* to mind, but now his fur was so sparkling clean and well-brushed, just a speck of mud or a clinging leaf would spoil it. He was quite worn out from the hard work of keeping clean by the time he reached the bridge. But somebody was lying in wait for him.

'Got you!' said an angry voice when Jago ducked under the bridge. 'Now I'll teach you to steal my billy-goats!'

And it all went dark as a sack came down over the terrified troll's head.

The Well-dressed Troll
5

Farmer Jenkins was in a fine mood.

He had bagged his troll!

He whistled as he tied a cord round the top of the sack. The sack wriggled and squirmed. 'Keep still,' Farmer Jenkins told it.

Inside the sack Jago thought hard.

Farmer Jenkins heard a muffled voice. 'You made a mistake. You have caught the wrong person!'

'No mistake,' said the farmer cheerfully. 'You're the goat-stealing troll, and now I've caught you at last, I shan't let you go!'

'I'm not,' insisted the sack. 'I'm somebody else entirely.'

The farmer paused. His sister Bettina had given him the tip-off about the troll under the bridge. It couldn't be anyone else, unless young Gaye had come back this way to look for the troll. 'If you were Gaye,' said the farmer out loud, 'You would have a pony-tail.'

'Loosen the knot,' said Jago, 'and you'll see.'

So the farmer loosened the cord, and Jago pushed out the end of his tail.

In the dark under the bridge it felt very like a pony-tail. But Farmer Jenkins was still suspicious.

'If you were Gaye,' said the farmer, 'you'd have something to brush your pony-tail with.'

'Loosen the knot a bit more,' said Jago, 'and you'll see.'

So, the farmer opened the sack a little more and Jago pushed out the hairbrush Gaye had given him.

Farmer Jenkins frowned. It was certainly a hairbrush. He thought of one more test.

'If you were Gaye,' he thought aloud, 'I'd know you by the perfume you wear.'

'Loosen the knot a bit more,' said Jago. 'Put your nose to the hole, and you'll see.'

So the farmer loosened the cord still

more, put his nose to the hole and sniffed. And it *was* Gaye's perfume!

But then Jago reached up and got hold of the farmer's nose and pulled it. He pulled it so hard that he pulled himself right out of the sack.

Then he snatched up his bundle and leapt up the bank, springing to the top on his strong troll legs.

He would have liked to explain that he really *wasn't* a goat-stealing troll, but a vegetarian. So it was true he was somebody else entirely, even if he wasn't Gaye. But it seemed a bad time for explaining. Furious at being tricked the farmer scrambled up the bank after him, holding his smarting nose.

Jago darted among a lot of shopping trolleys. Although it was getting dark the supermarket was still open. Jago raced towards some parked cars.

Farmer Jenkins lumbered after him but crashed into one of the trolleys. He toppled over and fell in it. The trolley began to move, not in a straight line, but round in circles, as supermarket trolleys always prefer to do.

The unfortunate farmer wriggled and heaved but he was stuck fast. He bellowed in fury as the trolley span round and round.

Scared by the farmer's shouting, Jago crouched behind a car. Farmer Jenkins struggled so hard that the trolley began to run back towards the stream.

Oh, dear! The trolley tipped over the edge, sending the farmer tumbling into the water below!

What a noise he made! Jago could tell Farmer Jenkins was very cross indeed. When Jago heard him climbing out of the stream, the troll knew he'd better find a

place to hide quickly!

Suddenly the car boot beside him sprang open like an enormous mouth. He must have pressed the knob without meaning to. A perfect place to hide! thought Jago, and he jumped inside and pulled it shut after him.

A few moments later, with a great roaring noise, the car began to move.

There was something quite soft and comfortable in the boot of the car, so Jago wrapped it round him in the dark and wondered where the car would take him. Far away from Farmer Jenkins, he hoped! Some people were not a bit friendly. But he felt sure Daniel and Dawn would be, now that he was a clean and tidy troll.

Or was he? His fur was in quite a mess again after that chase in the car park. He could feel it sticking out in all directions. Jago sighed. He took out Gaye's brush and started to do his fur all over again as best he could in the dark. It was such hard work keeping tidy!

Such hard work that Jago didn't notice the car stopping! When the boot opened and a large hand reached in to grab at him, it startled the troll so much that he leapt out of the boot past the big dark shape of the grabber.

He was in the driveway of a big house. Clutching his bundle Jago scuttled across a lawn and hid in some bushes at the far side.

Horrocks the butler was startled, too. He had only reached in to the boot and then – whoosh! A flash of green rushing across the lawn! What did it mean? He had better tell his mistress Lady Cynthia about this at once.

'Ah! Horrocks,' said her Ladyship, inside. 'Did you remember to fetch the green rug from the cleaners?'

'Yes, madam.'

'Good! Bring it in at once and put it back in front of the fire.'

'Er . . . I can't, your Ladyship.'

'You *can't?*' Lady Cynthia raised her eyebrows.

'Well . . . I hardly know how to explain it to your Ladyship . . .'

Lady Cynthia looked at him over her spectacles. 'Get on with it, Horrocks. Where's the rug?'

Horrocks took a deep breath. 'Your green rug just jumped out of the car boot, madam, and escaped into the bushes!'

'Horrocks,' said her Ladyship. 'My rug

has never shown any sign of moving before. It has never wriggled or crawled or strolled over to the window to take a look at the view. It has never so much as *twitched!* How could it suddenly jump up and run away?'

'I don't know, madam,' said Horrocks miserably.

Lady Cynthia thought for a moment. She trusted Horrocks. He was the perfect butler – always utterly reliable! So if Horrocks said her rug had escaped – then escaped it had! So she said, 'Well, don't just stand there! It's a valuable rug. It it's escaped, you'd better get after it at once.'

So Horrocks set off with a torch and searched the front garden. He shone the light under every bush and round every corner. There was no sign of the rug.

After a while Lady Cynthia came out to see how he was getting on. Passing the car she smelled a very strong perfume smell and looked inside. And there it was! Rather crumpled, but definitely there – the green rug!

'Horrocks!' she called. 'Look what I've found!' The butler came puffing and grunting out of the shrubbery. He stared at the rug in the light of his torch.

'It must have jumped back in again,' he said.

Lady Cynthia giggled. 'Nonsense, Horrocks! You've been seeing things!'

The butler went very red indeed.

Meanwhile Jago had wandered round the back of the big house. What wonderful lairs these people lived in! Jago admired the way they built them above the ground, instead of digging them out below as trolls did. Would he ever dare go inside one? He supposed not.

Lady Cynthia's wide lawns stretched down to a lake. The lake was narrow at one end and across the finger of water there was a beautiful ornamental bridge.

'It's perfect!' breathed Jago. 'Much better than that concrete one. Just the place to stay the night!' And the small troll crept under one end of the bridge, curled up on the grassy bank and fell fast asleep.

In the morning, a beam of sunshine slanted under the bridge and woke him. He opened his bundle and chose some tasty nuts and berries for breakfast.

It wasn't long before he heard footsteps on the boards overhead. Another chance to ask his question about the children! He leapt out from under the bridge.

'Who's that trip-trapping across MY bridge?' he roared.

Lady Cynthia jumped a foot in the air. 'Oh, my goodness!' she gasped. 'Until now I always thought it was *my* little bridge! Whatever are you?'

'My name's Jago and I'm a troll. Who are you?' said Jago.

'I'm Lady Cynthia. How do you do? So you're a troll! Then I suppose you mean to eat me up with all those sharp teeth of yours. I must say you look too small for the job – but I'm only a little old lady, so perhaps you could manage it.'

Jago laughed. 'I don't eat little old ladies. Don't worry. I'm a vegetarian troll and, anyway, I've *had* my breakfast. I only wanted to ask you a question.'

'Ask away,' said Lady Cynthia, sniffing in a puzzled way. What a powerful smell of perfume there was!

'I'm on my way to make friends with two children. The only trouble is, they don't like trolls much. What can I do to make them change their minds?'

Lady Cynthia thought about it.

'*I* know,' she said at last. 'If you want to make a good impression you have to wear smart clothes. You, I can't help noticing,

aren't wearing any clothes at all.'

Jago twitched his tail nervously. 'Do you really think I should?'

'No doubt about it,' said her Ladyship. 'I always take care to dress well myself.'

'You're certainly very elegant,' said the troll.

'Thank you. Now come with me. I've got just the thing for you.' She led the way to the garden shed. Hanging inside the door were some overalls. 'Try these – they're new. Horrocks was going to do his odd jobs in them, but you can have them. I'll leave you to put them on. Goodbye – and good luck with those children.'

'Thank you – thank you very much!' Jago called after her. Then he started to put on the overalls. This took a long time. Jago wasn't used to clothes, and it was many tries before he worked out which were the armholes and which the legholes. Then he got completely lost inside the overalls and thought he might never escape. But he *did* get it right in the end, and even fastened up the buttons in the right buttonholes.

Only now . . . he seemed to have lost his paws.

After another long struggle Jago managed to roll up the sleeves and the trouserlegs and found his paws again. A perfect fit! Well . . . more or less. What a lot there was to learn about making friends! Now he was quite exhausted.

Inside the big house, Horrocks served Lady Cynthia's morning coffee on a tray. He happened to glance out of the window. He made a sort of strangled noise and crashed the tray down on the coffee-table.

'What is it, Horrocks?' said the mistress.

'There . . . there's a green monster in the garden wearing . . . wearing *MY* overalls!'

Lady Cynthia's eyes twinkled and she

hid a smile. She knew perfectly well who was in the garden, but she *did* so like teasing Horrocks!

'Really, Horrocks,' she said. 'Have you started seeing impossible things again?'

Horrocks went twice as red as before. 'I'll prove it!' he shouted, and rushed out of the house determined to capture the monster and bring it back to Lady Cynthia in triumph . . .

The Very Polite Troll
6

Jago was admiring his smart new overalls when Horrocks burst out of the house and came running down the garden, angrily waving his arms.

'Oh, dear,' said Jago. 'He looks just like the farmer did yesterday. I think it's time I moved on!'

'Come back here with my stolen overalls, you thieving creature!' roared Horrocks.

But Jago streaked away towards the high garden wall. The troll made a powerful jump and got his paws on top of it. Just as he was about to swing himself over, he felt the butler's large hand grip his ankle, and his heart sank.

'Let go!' squealed Jago.

'No,' said Horrocks. 'I'm locking you up in my shed, to prove I didn't imagine you.'

Jago didn't want to be locked up. He thought quickly. 'But you did imagine me,' he said. 'I'm not *really* here.'

'What?' said the butler, startled. He held on tight to Jago's ankle.

'I'm just a figment of your imagination,' said the troll. 'How else would I know what you're thinking?'

'You don't know what I'm thinking,' said the butler uneasily.

'I do,' said Jago. 'You're thinking of a green, furry creature. Am I right?'

'Yes . . .' said Horrocks suspiciously.

'You're thinking it's got *your* overalls on!' Jago chuckled. 'Only a fine, strong imagination such as yours could dream that one up!'

'Thank you,' said Horrocks, rather pleased with the compliment.

'And you're imagining . . . oh, this is very good! . . . now you're even imagining the perfume the creature smells of!'

The butler wrinkled his nose. 'Why, so I am,' he said proudly.

'You know, with such a powerful imagination as yours, I bet you could even imagine me climbing down off this wall . . .'

Horrocks half closed his eyes. 'I can, it's true!'

'. . . and walking to the shed with you, as meek as a kitten . . .'

'Yes,' said the butler triumphantly. 'I've got it. There you go, meek as a kitten . . .'

'If you can make me do that by the strength of your imagination,' said Jago admiringly, 'you don't really need to hang on to my ankle, do you?'

'Of course not!' Horrocks laughed at the very idea. He let go of Jago's ankle at once.

Jago was up and over the wall in a flash.

Horrocks opened his eyes and gave a roar of fury.

'I told you I wasn't really there,' laughed Jago from the other side of the wall. 'And now I'm not!' But it wasn't safe to stay and talk; he could hear the butler crashing through the shrubbery to the gate; so Jago set off at his fastest lope.

Ten minutes later, Jago was almost out of puff. It was no joke, having to run in clothes! Far too hot! And the trouser legs kept unrolling and trying to trip him up. Horrocks was catching up. Unless the troll could dodge him soon, he was done for.

He came to a junction and turned the corner and ran slap into a crowd of people. Jago was scared. Would they catch him and hand him over to Horrocks? But no – the people seemed pleased to see him!

'Oh – what a marvellous costume!'

'A green monster – that's very good!'

'Who made your outfit? I can't even see the zip!'

'Thank you,' said Jago, thinking they were admiring his smart new overalls. The crowd swept him along. And what a strange crowd it was! There was a snowman marching along. There was a clown, and a Father Christmas. There was even a bear, and a gorilla! A long, lumpy creature went by with letters on its side that said it was the Loch Ness Monster.

No wonder nobody turned a hair at seeing Jago!

The snowman came up to him. 'Here, sonny, hold this!' It was a tin with a slot in the top. As Jago walked along, people by the side of the road put little round clinking things into the slot. 'Well done!' laughed the snowman.

Lots of the people wore T-shirts saying GRAND CHARITY WALK. Jago wasn't sure what that meant, but he began to feel very important as his tin filled up with clinking things.

Horrocks reached the corner. 'Where's that beast gone?' he gasped. But a flood of charity walkers poured by. 'Half of them are in animal costumes!' Horrocks realised

with dismay. 'There's no chance of finding the one *I'm* after. When I get back, Lady Cynthia will laugh at me again for seeing things! But I did see a green monster – I really *did!*'

Jago lollopped along, happy to have escaped from Horrocks. But it was a pity he'd had to leave Lady Cynthia's bridge. He began to wonder if there *was* any place in the world a vegetarian troll could stay.

At least he'd learnt two important things to help him make friends with Daniel and Dawn: being clean and tidy was one, and wearing smart clothes was the other. Strange and surprising things for a troll to learn! How many more things were there still to discover?

A shadow fell over him and he looked up from his deep thoughts. He was alone! The walkers seemed to have turned off without his noticing. He slipped the collecting tin in his overall pocket. He was walking beside a great, wide river that made the little stream on Windy Moor seem like a trickle. And the shadow was caused by a bridge over the river.

What a mighty bridge it was! It arched high above him, and two great towers held it up as it soared across the valley.

Wouldn't it be something, thought Jago, to live under such a majestic bridge!

Well, perhaps he would! Why not? He grew excited at the thought of it. He'd be like a king amongst trolls with such a bridge!

But how would he ever leap up on top of it? He tried a few leaps. His strong legs thrust him high into the air – but not nearly high enough. Jago chuckled. 'I'd need wings to get up there!' He began to climb the steep bank instead.

After a while he was almost up to the deck of the bridge. He could hear the whoosh of cars going past. He decided to give the usual shout, just to show the world it was *his* bridge now.

He put up his head and roared, 'Who's that trip-trapping across MY bridge?'

To his surprise a head peered over the parapet. It belonged to a man with a blue peaked cap.

'Who said that?' asked the man.

'It was me,' said Jago. 'Jago – the troll.' He put a leg over the parapet. 'Who are you?'

'I'm Bill, the toll-bridge man. I collect the money from the cars that use the bridge. Are you the sort of troll that eats people up?'

'No,' said Jago. 'I'm a vegetarian troll.'

'Good,' said Bill.

'Can I ask you a question?' said Jago.

'Go ahead,' said Bill.

'I want to make friends with two children who don't like trolls. How can I change their minds?'

'That's easy,' said Bill. 'Stop yelling "Who's that trip-trapping across MY bridge?" It's very alarming. In fact, it's downright rude! It would certainly frighten children. You should be much more polite.'

'Oh!' said Jago. 'What should I say?'

'Well, how about, "Excuse me. Would you mind telling me your name, please?" or "Good afternoon. Glad to meet you. I'm Jago." That kind of thing goes down much better.'

Jago blinked his enormous eyes in confusion. The bridge-cry had always been the same. Trolls had used those words for centuries. He'd never thought of saying anything different. But now he could see that it might sound rude, or even frightening. It was clear he'd have to learn to be more polite.

'All right,' said Jago. 'Let me have a practice.' So he climbed back over the parapet, and called out, 'Excuse me! Good afternoon! Would you please tell me your name?'

It didn't have the same *ring* about it as the old words somehow. But Bill was pleased.

'That's fine,' the toll-man smiled. 'Would you like to see my kiosk?'

'Thank you. That is very kind of you,' said Jago politely.

Bill's kiosk was a little cabin in the middle of the road. They went inside. Bill let Jago put on his peaked cap, and sit on the stool by the window. They had a chat. Jago told Bill he'd decided to live under this bridge, and dig a lair underneath as soon as he got round to it, and Bill said that was all right with him, as long as he could keep doing his job in his kiosk on the top. Bill was sitting in a comfortable chair at the back of the kiosk and all this chatting seemed to be making him tired, for after a while his chin fell on to his chest and he began to snooze.

Jago was wondering what to do next when a car came by and stopped by the window, which had a gap in it. The driver's hand reached up to the gap. 'Here,' said the driver, and plonked down some of those little round clinking things, then the car drove off.

'Thank you,' said Jago. He knew what to

do with the silver and brown things. He took his tin out of his pocket. He put the round things in the slot.

Every few minutes the same thing happened, until the tin was full, and then Jago found a brown leather bag and began to fill that. The drivers saw his peaked cap, and never noticed that his face was any different from the usual toll-man's.

When there was a quiet moment, Jago climbed out of the kiosk. Outside there was a board with words chalked on it: STOP AND PAY THE TOLL. He looked at the words for a while. Then, fetching a piece of chalk he'd noticed in the kiosk, he made one small change. Now the sign said: STOP AND PAY THE TROLL.

Jago liked that much better. He went back to collecting the jingly stuff at the window until a car came by with the snowman driving it.

'Ho-ho,' said Jago. 'Have you finished walking?'

'Oh, hello,' said the snowman. 'Yes, but we didn't collect as much money as I hoped.'

'Do you mean this jingly stuff?' asked Jago. 'What do you want it for?'

'To help the sick children at the hospital,'

answered the snowman.

That sounded a very good idea indeed to Jago, so he handed over the heavy tin, and the bulging leather bag too.

'That's marvellous,' said the snowman. 'This will make all the difference. You're a wonder, you've collected more than anyone else!' And he drove away.

Jago felt very pleased. He turned round and saw that Bill had woken up, and was staring at him with a look of fury. Whatever was the matter with him?

'What have you done?' Bill shouted. 'You thief, you've stolen the toll-money and given it to your partner, the villain in that car! I'll lose my job over this!'

Bill leapt up from his easy chair and made a grab for the troll. That was enough for Jago! He had no idea why Bill was so cross. It was just like Farmer Jenkins and Horrocks all over again! Jago knew what *that* meant. He knew what he had to do.

He burst out of the kiosk and ran for his life.

Jago tore across the bridge with the angry toll-man puffing close behind him. 'I'm on the run again!' thought the troll ruefully. 'I'm getting quite used to it!'

At the other end of the bridge was the main street of town, with shops on either side, and there were cars and people going up and down. Jago ran along the pavement.

'Stop that thief!' yelled Bill behind him. Some of the people turned and came towards Jago. What could he do? He remembered how Grandfather used to scare people away from the lair. Could he do it too? He bared his sharp teeth in a ferocious snarl. The people backed away from him hastily. It worked! The troll got through to the end of Main Street, and turned a corner. Now he was in a road that was mostly houses.

But the toll-man was behind him still. Jago looked left and right as he ran, for somewhere to hide. At last there was an alley between two houses. The troll dived into the alley. Crash! He ran slap into some dustbins, sending them rolling in all directions.

That gave Jago an idea. He picked up one dustbin that was empty. He turned it upside down. He climbed up on another, and stood on its lid. He waited until Bill came hurtling round the corner of the alley.

Jago jammed the plastic dustbin down over Bill's head and shoulders.

Bill staggered, amazed to be suddenly in the dark with his arms pinned at his sides. He bounced off a wall, only to hit the one opposite. He shouted angrily when he nearly lost his balance and tripped over.

Jago only heard a muffled noise from the dustbin. When he was sure it was safe, the troll climbed down. Gently he turned Bill round, and with a little push set him going along the pavement back towards Main Street. Jago smiled. People were staring out

of their windows at the walking dustbin as it went by. Someone would soon come out and help Bill, the troll hoped. Meanwhile he had his chance to get away.

Big drops of rain began to fall as Jago lollopped down the alley, coming out on to a sports field. Where to go now? The rain came harder and a gust of wind ruffled Jago's fur. He'd better find somewhere to shelter.

All this running had made the young troll

very tired. These people were very puzzling
– one minute helping him in his quest to
make friends with Daniel and Dawn, the
next minute chasing him all over town!
Would he ever understand them? He
remembered what the old trolls said:
'People and trolls don't mix!' Perhaps they
were right after all. Maybe a vegetarian troll
didn't belong anywhere!

Jago's shoulders drooped. He felt very
dejected. The rain drummed on the field all
round him.

'I know this place!' he said suddenly.
'The sports field – this rose-hedge – that
garden with the swing and the summer-
house – this is where Daniel and Dawn
live!'

And so it was.

The summer-house! Just the place to
shelter!

Jago made for the rose-hedge and peered
through. The windows of the house stared
blankly back at him: nobody seemed to be
in. He'd better make up his mind or he'd
soon be drenched.

He slipped through the rose-hedge and
with two quick lopes reached the summer-
house. He went inside and pulled the door
shut behind him.

It was warm and dry inside. Jago felt quite cosy watching rain streaming down the windows and listening to the roaring of the wind outside.

'The time has come for me to meet Daniel and Dawn,' he said. 'Didn't I say I'd come back one day? And here I am!' It was an exciting thought. But the thought made him nervous, too, when he remembered the story of the Billy-goats Gruff, and the troll who was the villain of the story. Would the children think *he* was a villain?

No! Not any more! He'd asked the people he'd met about making friends, and he'd learned the right way to do it.

The children would be glad to see such a clean, smart, polite troll.

He practised to himself the polite things he was going to say.

He thrust a paw into his overalls pocket. Good! Gaye's brush was there. He brushed his fur until it shone.

He brushed down his overalls to get rid of every speck of dirt picked up that long day. Oh dear! His feet were dirtiest of all. He brushed them too, until they were spotless.

And when he'd done all that he yawned a very wide yawn showing all his sharp teeth. Then he curled up on a wooden seat and fell asleep.

The storm was so loud in the night that the twins woke. They crept into their mother's bedroom. 'It's so noisy!' they said. 'Can we sleep with you, Mum?'

'Come on, then,' she said. So they all snuggled down together.

In the morning the storm was over, but the garden was a sea of mud, and a branch had broken off the apple tree, and part of the fence had blown down. 'What a mess!' the children said when they looked out. 'Let's go and explore the garden.'

They played a game of balancing along the fallen apple-tree branch, and then Dawn said, 'Let's go in the summer-house,' so they did. And there inside was a small, green creature, fast asleep.

'It's *him!*' shrieked Daniel. 'It's the troll! I knew he'd come back!'

'Shush, Daniel,' said Dawn. 'You'll frighten him.'

Jago snapped awake. His enormous eyes blinked at the two children. He'd slept right through the night! And now here were the twins already. It was the moment he'd been waiting for.

He got to his feet, smoothed down his overalls proudly, and said: 'Good morning! I am Jago, the vegetarian troll. I am very pleased to meet you. I hope we can be friends!'

Daniel and Dawn looked at each other, and then they looked back at Jago.

'Are you *sure* you're a troll?' said Dawn, with a puzzled look.

'He *must* be a troll,' said Daniel. 'Just look at his face! But why's he wearing *clothes?*'

'Trolls don't wear clothes,' Dawn agreed. 'Not in our story book.'

'You're right,' said Daniel. 'They have a coat of fur already. What would a troll want clothes for?'

Dawn said, '*I* thought a troll would be all muddy. Because of living under bridges.'

'I don't think a troll should smell of perfume,' said Daniel.

'The trolls in the book are *never* polite,' said Dawn. 'They always roar and bellow and say things like . . .'

Both the children cried together: 'Who's that trip-trapping across MY bridge!'

'You see,' said Daniel to Jago, 'We were hoping to meet . . .'

'. . . a *proper* troll!' Dawn finished.

'But I AM a proper troll!' Jago burst out

indignantly. And he suddenly remembered his mother Frith saying, "Be sure not to forget you're a troll." Jago grinned foolishly. What a twit he'd been! He *had* forgotten he was a troll.

He looked down at himself in dismay.

What a nuisance it had been to keep his fur brushed all the time!

How hot and stuffy it was in these overalls!

How he'd missed the joyful ring of the bridge-cry!

Jago smiled. He asked the twins: 'Would you be friends with me if I got muddy again? And took off these overalls? And roared and bellowed like a proper troll?'

'Of *course* we will!' said the twins in chorus.

Jago's smile grew wider and wider. He unbuttoned the overalls and pulled them off. What a relief *that* was!

He looked at the muddy puddles left by the rainstorm. They were very tempting!

He lollopped over to the biggest, wettest one.

He jumped in it with both feet.

Then, with a cry of delight, he rolled in it.

And he yelled: 'Who's that trip-trapping across MY bridge?'

Daniel and Dawn laughed. 'Now we *know* you're a proper troll!' they said.

Good News and Bad
8

A fine game of Bridges was soon going strong in the garden. Jago crouched under the climbing frame shouting, 'Who's that trip-trapping over MY bridge?' and the twins ran away squealing as Jago lollopped after them. And then the twins took turns at being the troll and Daniel chased Jago and Dawn, and then Dawn chased Daniel and Jago.

'Have you ever been on a swing?' asked Dawn. Jago shook his head. 'Come on then!'

Dawn showed him how to hold the ropes with his paws and kick his legs forward and back to make the swing go. Jago soon got

the idea. It felt wonderful! It was like flying. Jago felt very happy. This was just what he had dreamed of when he first came down from Windy Moor and spotted the children.

They played all morning. At the end of it they were firm friends. Daniel showed Jago the tuft of green fur he'd left behind on the night of the story.

'I thought you wouldn't want to meet a troll, when I heard that story,' said Jago.

'That was only a story,' said Daniel. 'We're very excited to meet a *real* troll.'

'And you're just the kind *I* wanted to meet,' said Dawn. 'A vegetarian one, that won't want to eat me up!'

'So I can make friends among people, and still be a proper troll!' said Jago happily.

Mrs O'Brien came out of the house just then.

'We've got a new friend, Mum,' said the twins.

'That's nice,' she said absently.

'He's a troll, Mum,' said the twins.

'Oh, good,' she said, folding up a letter she'd been reading and putting it away in her pocket.

'Mum!' laughed Dawn. 'We said a *troll!*'

'Oh!' gasped Mrs O'Brien, as it sank in what Dawn had said. 'A troll! You mean *the* troll we saw slipping through the hedge . . . ?'

'Yes!' squealed the twins. 'He's called Jago.'

Mrs O'Brien looked amazed as she shook paws with him. 'So you were right, Daniel. There really are trolls nowadays. It's an honour to meet you, Jago.'

Proudly the twins each took hold of one of their new friend's muddy green paws.

'He went to a lot of trouble before coming to see us,' explained Dawn. 'He got all clean and tidy and he put clothes on and he learned to speak politely, just for us.'

'I thought it was the right way to make friends,' said Jago.

'Oh, no,' said Mrs O'Brien. 'The right way to make friends is to be yourself. Real friends will like you just as you are.'

How lucky he was to have found such friends! thought Jago.

'I've had such a lot of fun,' said the young troll, 'but I must be going, if I'm to find a bridge to sleep under tonight.'

'Have you no home to go to, Jago?' frowned Mrs O'Brien.

'I'm a homeless troll,' admitted Jago; and he began to tell his new friends all about his adventures. How each time he'd found a bridge, along came someone trying to catch him, and how he'd ended up having to run away.

'You poor thing!' cried Dawn.

'What an awful time you've had!' said Daniel.

Their mother was cross to hear of Jago's misfortunes. 'When some people meet a thing they don't understand,' she said, 'they can't bear to let it go free.'

'What about your family, Jago?' asked Dawn. 'Can't you go home to them?'

Jago shook his head. 'When I decided to be a vegetarian, there was all sorts of trouble. That's why I had to leave home in the first place.'

Mrs O'Brien gave a start. A vegetarian! That reminded her of something she had read in that letter. She pulled it out of her pocket.

'Listen,' she said. 'I had a letter from Mr Wise in Australia this morning.'

'He's our next-door neighbour,' said Daniel to Jago. 'Mum's been looking after his house while he's away.'

'This is what it says,' Mrs O'Brien went on. '"Dear Mrs O'Brien, I have decided to stay in Australia for good. I won't be needing my house any more. I leave it to you to decide who should live there – perhaps some poor homeless creature with nowhere to go. And I would like to think you will choose someone who is a vegetarian like myself. I'm sure you will know when the right one comes along. Love from your good friend, Mr Wise."'

'It's been worrying me all morning,' said the twins' mother. 'How would I find the right person? And then *you* come along, Jago! A homeless creature with nowhere to go! *And* a vegetarian!'

'It's as if Mr Wise *knew* Jago would turn up,' said Dawn.

'He's exactly what the letter says!' cried Daniel.

'Yes,' said his mum. 'And what's more, Mr Wise doesn't say a word about *people* moving in. He doesn't say it has to be a person at all. He actually wrote "creature". I reckon that settles it.'

They all turned to Jago with wide smiles.

'I don't understand,' stammered the troll. 'Has the letter got anything to do with me?'

'Jago,' said Mrs O'Brien, 'Would you like to live in a *house*?'

Jago could hardly believe it. The O'Briens took him next door to see Mr Wise's house.

He was speechless as they walked inside. He – a troll – going in one of the wonderful above-the-ground lairs that the people lived in! He remembered looking down at them from the Moor, at night when they were all lit up. And now he was inside one himself.

He marvelled at the rooms, every one bigger than a single lair! And the windows, that let so much light in but kept the cold wind out! Once he found his voice there were so many questions to ask. What were the kitchen and the bathroom for? How did you work the doors? Did people really sleep in *beds*? It was all amazing and exciting.

'Well, Jago,' said Mrs O'Brien at last. 'This is now your house – if you want it, that is.'

'Come and live next door to us, Jago!' said Dawn.

'We can play every day!' urged Daniel.

A lump came into the troll's throat. How kind the O'Briens were being to him! Could it be true – could he really live here?

An hour later, after they'd all gone back to Daniel and Dawn's house and eaten a delicious meal – vegetarian, in Jago's honour – he managed at last to believe his luck, and said yes – he *would* come and live in the house next door. The children were delighted. Probably nobody else in the whole world had a troll who lived next door! Their mother was very pleased too. 'You've solved my problem and saved me a lot of worry,' she told Jago. 'And we like you very much, and will be proud to be your neighbours.'

Jago beamed at them all. He thanked them for being so kind to him. Then suddenly he thought of his mother anxiously waving him goodbye, and the promise he'd made to let her know when he'd found some friends and a place to live.

'What's the matter, Jago?' Daniel had noticed the troll's troubled look.

'I have to go back and tell my mother,' said Jago. 'I must let her know I've found a new lair.'

'Of course you must,' agreed Mrs O'Brien. So they all got up to see him off, waving to him as he climbed through the rose-hedge, promising to be back soon.

Jago stood by the river bank, horrified. During the night the heavy rain had swelled the streams into a raging river. The overflowing water had torn chunks out of the banks, uprooting bushes and small trees, and sent them rushing downstream

in the fierce current.

At the bridge the angry water had battered at the old bricks, and sucked away the crumbling mortar that held the bricks together, until the weakened bridge had given up and collapsed.

Where the trolls' lair had been only a sad heap of bricks and stones remained, half under a wide pool of flood water.

Of Jago's family, there was no sign at all.

A New Lair
9

Jago searched everywhere beside the swollen stream, calling for his lost family. What if they were gone forever, and he would never see them again? He was frantic with worry, and his voice grew hoarse from calling. And then suddenly he stumbled into a hollow in the ground left by a tree uprooted in the storm. And there they were! Sheltering among the roots of the fallen tree – all of them, alive and safe, his parents Frith and Obrak, baby Korta, and Grandma and Grandfather too!

'Thank goodness you're safe!' cried Jago, as they all gathered round and hugged him. Even little Korta gurgled at her brother and tried to poke a happy finger in his eye.

'Thank goodness *you* are,' said Frith. 'I was afraid I'd never see you again. A terrible thing's happened – our lair has gone! Our lovely home! And now we have nowhere to live.'

Obrak hugged Jago, too, thumping him affectionately with a massive paw. 'I'm glad you're back, son,' he said gruffly. 'If it wasn't for me making such a fuss about eating up your dinner, you'd never have gone away. That stupid temper of mine! Will you forgive me?'

'Oh, yes, Father,' said Jago.

'Now we're *all* homeless. The lair's destroyed! Ours was the only hump-backed bridge for miles around. It will be a long, weary journey for us to find a new one!'

'If only you could come and live with me!' cried Jago.

'You?' Obrak stared. 'Have you found a bridge, then?'

'Better than that!' said Jago.

'Nothing *could* be better than a cosy lair under a hump-backed bridge,' shivered Grandma.

'*This* is,' Jago insisted. 'You see, my new home is – a house!'

'A house?' everyone exclaimed.

'The youngster's mad,' said Grandfather.

Jago explained. He told them about his kind new friends who wanted him to come and live in the empty house next door. 'But only vegetarians can live there,' he ended. 'It's a pity you aren't vegetarian, or you could all come and live there with me.'

Obrak chuckled. He reached into the tangled roots behind him, and from a hiding place he pulled out a bunch of leaves. He bit off a big mouthful and munched it. To his amazement Jago saw the others doing the same! Even Grandfather was cramming pawfuls of berries into his mouth.

'You see, Jago,' his mother explained, 'I gathered some of your kind of food from the woods and we all tried it. Everyone asked for more! So, you see, we're all vegetarians now!' Jago was delighted. 'Then you *can* come and live with me!'

The troll family talked it over. 'Mud!' said Grandma. 'That's the important thing. Is there plenty of mud at this house of yours?'

'Oodles of it!' Jago grinned.

It was really baby Korta who settled the matter. She gave a most fearsome sneeze and made them all jump.

'That does it,' said Frith. 'The baby's got

to have somewhere warm and dry – and quickly. Thank goodness you *have* found somewhere for us to live, Jago. Just lead the way!'

And so it was that a strange procession wound its way into the O'Briens' road an hour later, as the little party of trolls came to see their new home.

Jago led the way. Then came Obrak, glowering fiercely to left and right, ready to defend his family in case of any attack. Frith followed carrying baby Korta in her arms. Last came the old ones, Grandfather and Grandma, clutching each other's paws to keep their courage up, gazing fearful and wide-eyed at the tall houses.

'Oh, Jago!' squealed Grandma. 'The houses are staring at me with their square, shiny eyes!'

'They aren't eyes, but windows, Grandma,' explained Jago.

'This hard black soil hurts my feet,' complained Grandfather.

'It's not soil, but a road, Grandfather,' said Jago.

'Windows and roads!' marvelled his mother. 'What a strange new land we are in!'

And then there *were* eyes at the windows,

as the people in the houses peered out curiously at their new, furry neighbours.

'Will they attack?' said Obrak. 'I shall fight to the death!'

'It's all right, Father – they're just curious. They're not used to us yet.' But the eyes made Jago nervous, too, and he was glad to see the twins and Mrs O'Brien rush out of their house to greet them.

'Hello again, Jago!' said Mrs O'Brien. She waved towards the peering neightbours. 'I told everyone you're coming. They all agree it will be exciting to have someone really different like you in the street. They are dying to meet you. And this must be your family!'

'Yes! They are all vegetarian now, and they've lost their home in the flood,' said Jago. 'Can they come and live next door too?'

'Of course they can!' said Mrs O'Brien, and shook all their paws.

'Just a moment,' boomed a voice.

'Oh, no,' sighed Mrs O'Brien. 'I forgot to tell Mr Pyke!'

Seeing Mrs O'Brien with the strange visitors, some of the neighbours dared to come outside for a closer look. At the head of this small group was Mr Pyke.

Mr Pyke was Co-ordinator of the Neighbourhood Watch. He was Chairman of the Residents' Association. Mr Pyke liked to know everything that went on in his road. He did *not* like anything to happen in the road without his permission!

Mr Pyke boomed again. 'Are you responsible for these creatures?'

'No, I'm not,' retorted Mrs O'Brien. 'They're responsible for themselves.'

'I don't want to interfere,' said Mr Pyke (in his most interfering voice), 'but we can't have wild animals on the loose in the neighbourhood. I'm sure you realise that.'

The twins' mother squared up to Mr Pyke. 'Look here – you've no right to call my troll friends wild animals.'

'Trolls? Did you say *trolls?*'

'I did,' answered Mrs O'Brien defiantly. 'And as Jago here is the new owner of Mr Wise's house, he is now your neighbour, so the sooner you get used to him, the better!'

A murmur of excited talk broke out. Alarmed voices said, 'Trolls? Coming to live *here?* We can't have that!'

Mr Pyke turned away to talk to his supporters. Soon he said:

'Mrs O'Brien, none of us have seen trolls before, but we all read stories about them when we were young. They are dangerous creatures, I believe, who leap out from their hiding places to gobble up goats or even people. You only have to look at them to see how fierce they are. These people will not feel safe as long as your trolls are in our road.'

Obrak gave an annoyed snarl at this point, and everyone stepped back hastily.

Jago thought he'd better try and calm things down.

'Ladies and gentlemen,' he began. 'You've nothing to fear from us. Perhaps we trolls were once dangerous, but now it's different. We're respectable trolls, and what's more, we're vegetarian; so we're not planning to eat any of you!'

Daniel and Dawn said their bit too. 'We found Jago – and he's our friend,' they said.

The neighbours stared at Jago, wondering what to make of him. They didn't look much friendlier!

Things were looking bad – until Mr Pyke, who was standing closest, felt a sudden tug at his sleeve.

He gave a start. 'What – who did that?' he stammered.

Looking up at him from Frith's arms, a merry little face gurgled at Mr Pyke; a face with a cute fringe of beautiful, pale green fur; big, friendly turquoise eyes; a little snub nose not old enough to have grown sharp and pointy yet; and two teeth, one a tiny fang only just peeping out under her top lip.

And something magical happened: Mr Pyke's heart melted.

He bent down to Korta, whose little fist was tugging at his sleeve, and gave her a finger to hold instead, and the two of them cooed and gurgled at each other in baby talk.

'What a beautiful baby!' said Mr Pyke, in

quite the soppiest voice Dawn had ever heard. 'Is it, er, a boy-troll or a girl-troll?'

'Korta's a girl-troll,' answered Frith, beaming with pride.

'What a lovely baby sister you've got, Jago!' said Dawn.

'Have I?' blinked Jago. 'Yes, I suppose I have!'

'May I – do you think I could hold her?' asked the entranced Mr Pyke and, given permission, took Korta carefully and set off towards the O'Briens' house.

'Make way there,' he said severely to his astonished henchmen. Then he seemed to remember himself a little, and paused to announce:

'We'll all be generous in welcoming our new neighbours, I hope. That's only the decent thing to do, is it not?'

Then he left them, open-mouthed, behind, and led the way into the O'Brien's front door.

And then they all had tea.

The next morning Jago stepped proudly out of his own front door. He was carrying a hammer and some nails and a sign reading 'The Lair' which he set about fixing to the wall.

The young troll had got his wish and made friends with Daniel and Dawn. On top of that – who'd have thought it? – he'd brought his family to live amongst the people of the town! Trolls and people *could* mix, after all! It was a great step in the history of troll-kind, Jago was sure. A wonderful new experiment! Who could tell where it might lead? Perhaps one day, there'd be troll shops in Main Street! Troll teachers, and artists, and scientists! Maybe even a troll prime minister!

He stepped back to admire his new sign – and bumped into Grandma.

'You're out early, Grandma! What are you up to?'

She was carrying a heavy bucket of soil. Jago noticed there was a big hole in the middle of the front lawn.

'Never you mind,' retorted the old lady troll.

'Let me help,' Jago offered.

'I can manage,' said Grandma, struggling past him into the house with the heavy bucket. Jago followed curiously as she began puffing her way upstairs.

Half-way upstairs there came a voice: 'Who's that trip-trapping over MY bridge?' Jago leaned over the bannisters in surprise.

Salvatroll
Dali

10

Grandfather poked his grizzled head out from the cupboard under the stairs.

'It's only us, Grandfather,' said Jago. 'It's not your bridge, it's the stairs! Why are you lurking in there anyway? Don't you like your bedroom?'

'It feels more like a proper lair,' explained the old troll. 'Can't get used to beds at my age!'

Jago suddenly realised Grandma was disappearing into the bathroom. He raced after her before she could lock the door, a trick she had learned in no time.

Jago looked in. There was Grandma, stepping into the bath, which was half full of soil. The taps were on, and Grandma was stirring the mixture with a wooden spoon from the kitchen.

'Mud!' she exclaimed happily. 'My mud-bath's nearly ready!'

Jago laughed. Grandma and Grandfather were settling in well after all! *They* knew how to carry on being proper trolls, even in a strange new place. Everything was working out perfectly.

He sighed contentedly. Just then the doorbell rang and Jago jumped up with excitement to go down and answer it. That would be his friends Daniel and Dawn – his new *human* friends – coming round to play.